My Steps

by SALLY DERBY

illustrated by

ADJOA J. BURROWES

Lee & Low Books Inc. • New York

Printed in Hong Kong by South China Printing Co. (1988) Ltd.

Book design by Christy Hale
Book production by Our House

The text is set in Mixage Medium.
The illustrations are rendered using a cut-paper collage technique
that also incorporates watercolor and dyes.

10 9 8 7 6 5 4 3 2 1
First Edition

Library of Congress Cataloging-in-Publication Data
Derby, Sally
My steps/by Sally Derby; illustrated by Adjoa J. Burrowes.—1st ed.
p. cm.
Summary: A young Afro-American girl describes her favorite
playground—the front steps of her home on which she and her
friends play and experience the changing seasons.
ISBN: 1-880000-40-7
[1. Play—Fiction. 2. Seasons—Fiction. 3. Afro-Americans—Fiction.]
I. Burrowes, Adjoa J., ill. II. Title.
PZ7.M63343My   1996
[E]—dc20   96-33847
CIP AC

THESE ARE MY STEPS,
all five of them.
One, Two, Three, Four, Five.
I can hop up from One to Five
and down from Five to One
on just one foot.

Whenever it's a pretty day
I play on my steps
while cars and buses
swoosh down the street
and people walk by on the sidewalk.
Sometimes I know the people,
and then I say, "Morning, Mrs. Johnson,"
"Afternoon, Preacher Jones."
But my mom always says,
"Don't you go talking to strangers,"
so I don't. I look away.

At the top of my steps is the stoop
where I play with my friend, Essie.
Every morning before Essie comes
I bring the broom out
and I sweep away all the dirt
and the ants and the bugs
and the glass, if some
got broken in the night.

My stoop has sides,
two walls made of bricks.
When I was five, I couldn't see over them.
Now I'm so big, those walls
are only up to here on me.

Sometimes, when my mom's not looking,
we stand on the horses' backs,
like the lady in the circus.

Springtime mornings, my steps are shady,
cool and hard and smooth.
If I lie on the top step
all down my back I feel shivery-cool.
If I lie on my stomach
I see crooked cracks in the cement.

I pretend the cracks are rivers.
Once I took a piece of green paper
and I tore it into little pieces
and I crumbled up the pieces
and made bushes
all along the rivers.

Essie and I like to color.
She sits on Two
and puts her paper on Three.
I sit on Four and put my paper on Five.
That way we each have our own desk,
just like in school.
But if we don't put away our crayons,
that old sun can melt them
so they stick to the steps.
It takes a lot of scraping
when crayons stick to cement.

Some days,
when the sun's so bright it makes me squint,
if I ask and ask, my mom brings out a blanket,
and hangs it from wall to wall.

Then Essie and I, we have a shady cave,
where we sit and tell secrets
so quietly
people walking by don't even know we're there.

I have another friend,
that's Nicholas,
and when he comes
we all play stone school.
Here's how we play: I'm teacher first,
because they're my steps.
I put my hands behind my back and
hide a little stone.
Then I put my hands out in front.
Essie and Nicholas sit on One,
(that's kindergarten),
and they take turns guessing which hand.
When they guess right, they get to
move up to first grade.
And whoever gets to fourth grade first
gets to be teacher next.

Sometimes on summer afternoons
when the cement is
hot through your shoes,
the firemen open up
the hydrant near my steps.
The water shoots out and
splashes down the street.
Kids I don't even know come running,
till my ears are full of
shouting and laughing.
We get our clothes wet
and our faces wet
and our hair wet
and we kick and splash and run
till the firemen close the hydrant.

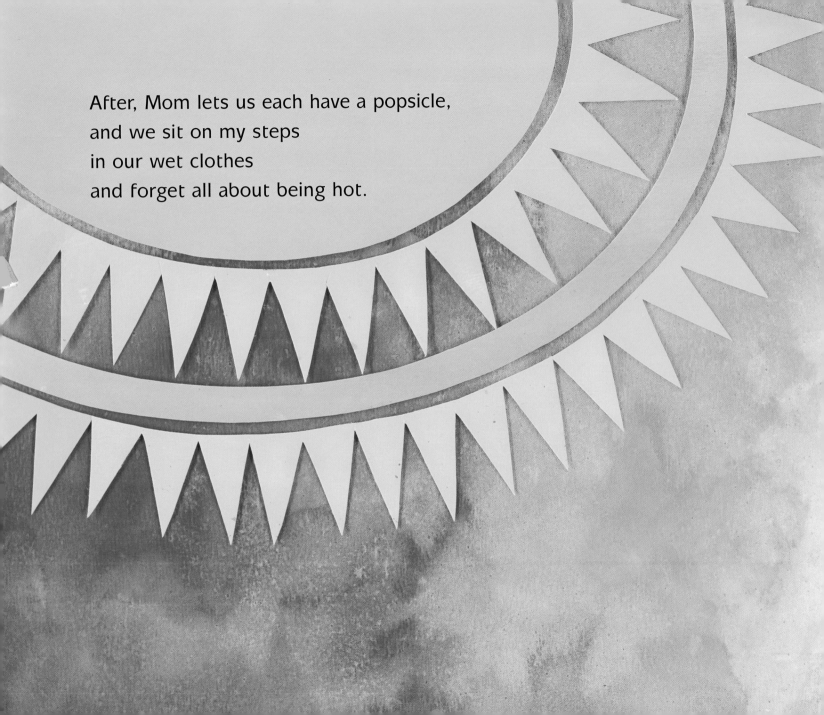

After, Mom lets us each have a popsicle,
and we sit on my steps
in our wet clothes
and forget all about being hot.

Summer is better than fall,
and hot is better than cold.
But I keep my steps clean
even when Mom says it's
too cold to play on them.
Before school I sweep away all the leaves.
If the leaves were wet,
I have leaf prints on my steps
like shadow leaves.
When I come home from school,
the leaf prints are gone,
but I have more leaves to sweep.

After fall, winter comes shivering in.
I shovel the snow and scrape the ice,
but that's hard.

When I finish, my mom says,
"Girl, let me feel that muscle."

Even in the winter,
I'm glad I have my steps,
all five of them,

and when I come back from Away,
I run up the steps like this...
OneTwoThreeFourFive,
and I push open the door and I shout

"I'M HOME!"